Selected Tales from
BEATRIX POTTER™

BEATRIX POTTER
The original and authorized editions

FREDERICK WARNE

Published by the Penguin Group
Penguin Books Ltd, 80 Strand, London WC2R 0RL, England
Penguin Young Readers Group, 345 Hudson Street, New York, New York 10014, USA
Penguin Group (Canada), 90 Eglinton Avenue East, Suite 700, Toronto, Ontario, Canada M4P 2Y3
Penguin Ireland, 25 St Stephen's Green, Dublin 2, Ireland
Penguin (Group) Australia, 250 Camberwell Road, Camberwell, Victoria 3124, Australia
Penguin Books India (P) Ltd, 11 Community Centre, Panchsheel Park, New Delhi 110 017, India
Penguin Group (NZ), cnr Airborne and Rosedale Roads, Albany, Auckland 1310, New Zealand
Penguin Books (South Africa) (Pty) Ltd, P O Box 9, Parklands 2121, South Africa

Penguin Books Ltd, Registered Offices: 80 Strand, London WC2R 0RL, England

Web site at: www.peterrabbit.com

First published by Frederick Warne 1986
This edition published 2007
1 3 5 7 9 10 8 6 4 2

ISBN 978 0 7232 5859 9

Printed in Malaysia

CONTENTS

THE TALE OF
PETER RABBIT

ONCE upon a time there were four little Rabbits, and their names were —

Flopsy,

Mopsy,

Cotton-tail,

and Peter.

They lived with their Mother in a sand-bank, underneath the root of a very big fir-tree.

"NOW my dears," said old Mrs. Rabbit one morning, "you may go into the fields or down the lane, but don't go into Mr. McGregor's garden. "Your Father had an accident there; he was put in a pie by Mrs. McGregor."

"NOW run along, and don't get into
mischief. I am going out."

THEN old Mrs. Rabbit took a basket and her umbrella, and went through the wood to the baker's. She bought a loaf of brown bread and five currant buns.

FLOPSY, Mopsy and Cotton-tail, who were good little bunnies, went down the lane to gather blackberries;

BUT Peter, who was very naughty, ran straight away to Mr. McGregor's garden, and squeezed under the gate!

FIRST he ate some lettuces and some French beans; and then he ate some radishes;

AND then, feeling rather sick, he went to look for some parsley.

BUT round the end of a cucumber frame, whom should he meet but Mr. McGregor!

MR. McGregor was on his hands and knees planting out young cabbages, but he jumped up and ran after Peter, waving a rake and calling out, "Stop thief!"

PETER was most dreadfully frightened; he rushed all over the garden,
for he had forgotten the way back to
the gate.

He lost one of his shoes among the
cabbages, and the other shoe amongst
the potatoes.

AFTER losing them, he ran on four legs and went faster, so that I think he might have got away altogether if he had not unfortunately run into a gooseberry net, and got caught by the large buttons on his jacket. It was a blue jacket with brass buttons, quite new.

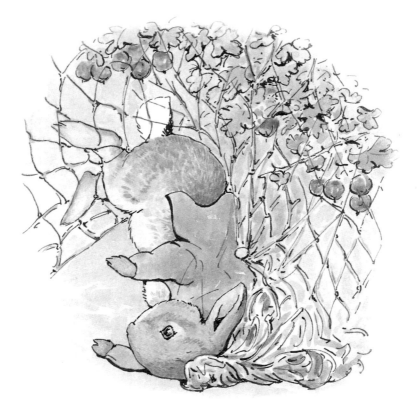

PETER gave himself up for lost, and shed big tears; but his sobs were overheard by some friendly sparrows, who flew to him in great excitement, and implored him to exert himself.

MR. McGregor came up with a
sieve, which he intended to pop
upon the top of Peter; but Peter
wriggled out just in time, leaving his
jacket behind him,

AND rushed into the tool-shed, and jumped into a can. It would have been a beautiful thing to hide in, if it had not had so much water in it.

M^R. McGregor was quite sure that Peter was somewhere in the tool-shed, perhaps hidden underneath a flower-pot. He began to turn them over carefully, looking under each.

Presently Peter sneezed —"Kerty-schoo!" Mr. McGregor was after him in no time,

AND tried to put his foot upon Peter, who jumped out of a window, upsetting three plants. The window was too small for Mr. McGregor, and he was tired of running after Peter. He went back to his work.

PETER sat down to rest; he was out of breath and trembling with fright, and he had not the least idea which way to go. Also he was very damp with sitting in that can.

After a time he began to wander about, going lippity — lippity — not very fast, and looking all round.

HE found a door in a wall; but it was locked, and there was no room for a fat little rabbit to squeeze underneath.

An old mouse was running in and out over the stone door-step, carrying peas and beans to her family in the wood. Peter asked her the way to the gate, but she had such a large pea in her mouth that she could not answer. She only shook her head at him. Peter began to cry.

THEN he tried to find his way straight across the garden, but he became more and more puzzled. Presently, he came to a pond where Mr. McGregor filled his water-cans. A white cat was staring at some gold-fish; she sat very, very still, but now and then the tip of her tail twitched as if it were alive. Peter thought it best to go away without speaking to her; he had heard about cats from his cousin, little Benjamin Bunny.

HE went back towards the tool-shed, but suddenly, quite close to him, he heard the noise of a hoe — scr-r-ritch, scratch, scratch, scritch. Peter scuttered underneath the bushes. But presently, as nothing happened, he came out, and climbed upon a wheel-barrow, and peeped over. The first thing he saw was Mr. McGregor hoeing onions. His back was turned towards Peter, and beyond him was the gate!

PETER got down very quietly off the wheelbarrow, and started running as fast as he could go, along a straight walk behind some blackcurrant bushes.

Mr. McGregor caught sight of him at the corner, but Peter did not care. He slipped underneath the gate, and was safe at last in the wood outside the garden.

MR. McGREGOR hung up the little jacket and the shoes for a scarecrow to frighten the blackbirds.

PETER never stopped running or looked behind him till he got home to the big fir-tree.

He was so tired that he flopped down upon the nice soft sand on the floor of the rabbit-hole, and shut his eyes. His mother was busy cooking; she wondered what he had done with his clothes. It was the second little jacket and pair of shoes that Peter had lost in a fortnight!

I AM sorry to say that Peter was not very well during the evening.

His mother put him to bed, and made some camomile tea; and she gave a dose of it to Peter!

"One table-spoonful to be taken at bed-time."

BUT Flopsy, Mopsy, and Cotton-tail
had bread and milk and blackberries for supper.

THE TALE OF
TIMMY TIPTOES

ONCE upon a time there was a little fat comfortable grey squirrel, called Timmy Tiptoes. He had a nest thatched with leaves in the top of a tall tree; and he had a little squirrel wife called Goody.

TIMMY TIPTOES sat out, enjoying the breeze; he whisked his tail and chuckled — "Little wife Goody, the nuts are ripe; we must lay up a store for winter and spring." Goody Tiptoes was busy pushing moss under the thatch — "The nest is so snug, we shall be sound asleep all winter." "Then we shall wake up all the thinner, when there is nothing to eat in spring-time," replied prudent Timothy.

WHEN Timmy and Goody Tiptoes
came to the nut thicket, they
found other squirrels were there
already.

Timmy took off his jacket and hung
it on a twig; they worked away quietly
by themselves.

EVERY day they made several
journeys and picked quantities of
nuts. They carried them away in bags,
and stored them in several hollow
stumps near the tree where they had
built their nest.

WHEN these stumps were full, they began to empty the bags into a hole high up a tree, that had belonged to a wood-pecker; the nuts rattled down — down — down inside.

"How shall you ever get them out again? It is like a money-box!" said Goody.

"I shall be much thinner before spring-time, my love," said Timmy Tiptoes, peeping into the hole.

THEY did collect quantities—
because they did not lose them!
Squirrels who bury their nuts in the
ground lose more than half, because
they cannot remember the place.

The most forgetful squirrel in the
wood was called Silvertail. He began
to dig, and he could not remember.
And then he dug again and found
some nuts that did not belong to him;
and there was a fight. And other
squirrels began to dig — the whole wood
was in commotion!

UNFORTUNATELY, just at this time a flock of little birds flew by, from bush to bush, searching for green caterpillars and spiders. There were several sorts of little birds, twittering different songs.

The first one sang — "Who's bin digging-up *my* nuts? Who's-been-digging-up *my* nuts?"

And another sang — "Little bit-a-bread and-*no*-cheese! Little bit-a-bread an'-*no*-cheese!"

46

THE squirrels followed and listened.
The first little bird flew into the
bush where Timmy and Goody Tiptoes
were quietly tying up their bags, and
it sang — "Who's-bin digging-up *my*
nuts? Who's been digging-up *my*-nuts?"

Timmy Tiptoes went on with his
work without replying; indeed, the
little bird did not expect an answer. It
was only singing its natural song, and
it meant nothing at all.

BUT when the other squirrels heard that song, they rushed upon Timmy Tiptoes and cuffed and scratched him, and upset his bag of nuts. The innocent little bird which had caused all the mischief, flew away in a fright!

Timmy rolled over and over, and then turned tail and fled towards his nest, followed by a crowd of squirrels shouting — "Who's-been digging-up *my*-nuts?"

THEY caught him and dragged him
up the very same tree, where there
was the little round hole, and they
pushed him in. The hole was much
too small for Timmy Tiptoes' figure.
They squeezed him dreadfully, it was
a wonder they did not break his ribs.
"We will leave him here till he con-
fesses," said Silvertail Squirrel, and he
shouted into the hole —

"Who's-been-digging-up *my*-nuts?"

TIMMY TIPTOES made no reply;
he had tumbled down inside the
tree, upon half a peck of nuts belonging
to himself. He lay quite stunned and
still.

GOODY TIPTOES picked up the
nut bags and went home. She made
a cup of tea for Timmy; but he didn't
come and didn't come.

Goody Tiptoes passed a lonely and
unhappy night. Next morning she ven-
tured back to the nut-bushes to look
for him; but the other unkind squirrels
drove her away.

She wandered all over the wood,
calling —

"Timmy Tiptoes! Timmy Tiptoes!
Oh, where is Timmy Tiptoes?"

IN the meantime Timmy Tiptoes
came to his senses. He found himself
tucked up in a little moss bed, very
much in the dark, feeling sore; it
seemed to be under ground. Timmy
coughed and groaned, because his ribs
hurted him. There was a chirpy noise,
and a small striped Chipmunk appeared
with a night light, and hoped
he felt better?

It was most kind to Timmy Tiptoes;
it lent him its night-cap; and the house
was full of provisions.

THE Chipmunk explained that it had rained nuts through the top of the tree — "Besides, I found a few buried!" It laughed and chuckled when it heard Timmy's story. While Timmy was confined to bed, it 'ticed him to eat quantities — "But how shall I ever get out through that hole unless I thin myself? My wife will be anxious!" "Just another nut — or two nuts; let me crack them for you," said the Chip-munk. Timmy Tiptoes grew fatter and fatter!

NOW Goody Tiptoes had set to
work again by herself. She did not
put any more nuts into the wood-pecker's
hole, because she had always
doubted how they could be got out
again. She hid them under a tree root;
they rattled down, down, down. Once
when Goody emptied an extra big
bagful, there was a decided squeak;
and next time Goody brought another
bagful, a little striped Chipmunk scram-
bled out in a hurry.

"IT is getting perfectly full-up down-
stairs; the sitting-room is full, and
they are rolling along the passage; and
my husband, Chippy Hackee, has run
away and left me. What is the expla-
nation of these showers of nuts?"

"I am sure I beg your pardon; I did
not know that anybody lived here," said
Mrs. Goody Tiptoes; "but where is
Chippy Hackee? My husband, Timmy
Tiptoes, has run away too." "I know
where Chippy is; a little bird told me,"
said Mrs. Chippy Hackee.

S HE led the way to the wood-pecker's tree, and they listened at the hole.

Down below there was a noise of nut crackers, and a fat squirrel voice and a thin squirrel voice were singing together —

"My little old man and I fell out,
How shall we bring this matter about?
Bring it about as well as you can,
And get you gone, you little old man!"

YOU could squeeze in, through that little round hole," said Goody Tiptoes. "Yes, I could," said the Chipmunk, "but my husband, Chippy Hackee, bites!"

Down below there was a noise of cracking nuts and nibbling; and then the fat squirrel voice and the thin squirrel voice sang —

"For the diddlum day
　Day diddle dum di!
　Day diddle diddle dum day!"

THEN Goody peeped in at the hole, and called down — "Timmy Tiptoes! Oh fie, Timmy Tiptoes!" And Timmy replied, "Is that you, Goody Tiptoes? Why, certainly!"

He came up and kissed Goody through the hole; but he was so fat that he could not get out.

Chippy Hackee was not too fat, but he did not want to come; he stayed down below and chuckled.

AND so it went on for a fortnight;
till a big wind blew off the top of
the tree, and opened up the hole and
let in the rain.

Then Timmy Tiptoes came out, and
went home with an umbrella.

B UT Chippy Hackee continued to
camp out for another week,
although it was uncomfortable.

AT last a large bear came walking
through the wood. Perhaps he also
was looking for nuts; he seemed to be
sniffing around.

CHIPPY HACKEE went home in a hurry!

AND when Chippy Hackee got
home, he found he had caught a
cold in his head; and he was more
uncomfortable still.

AND now Timmy and Goody Tiptoes
keep their nut-store fastened
up with a little padlock.

AND whenever that little bird sees the Chipmunks, he sings — "Who's-been-digging-up *my*-nuts? Who's been digging-up *my*-nuts?" But nobody ever answers!

THE TALE OF
THE PIE AND
THE PATTY-PAN

ONCE upon a time there was a Pussy-cat called Ribby, who invited a little dog called Duchess, to tea.

"Come in good time, my dear Duchess," said Ribby's letter, "and we will have something so very very nice. I am baking it in a pie-dish — a pie-dish with a pink rim. You never tasted anything so good! And *you* shall eat it all! *I* will eat muffins, my dear Duchess!" wrote Ribby.

Duchess read the letter and wrote an answer: "I will come with much pleasure at a quarter past four. But it is very strange. I was just going to invite you to come here, to supper, my dear Ribby, to eat something *most delicious*.

"I will come very punctually, my dear Ribby," wrote Duchess; and then at the end she added — "I hope it isn't mouse?"

THE INVITATION

And then she thought that did not look quite polite; so she scratched out "isn't mouse" and changed it to "I hope it will be fine," and she gave her letter to the postman.

But she thought a great deal about Ribby's pie, and she read Ribby's letter over and over again.

"I am dreadfully afraid it *will* be mouse!" said Duchess to herself— "I really couldn't, *couldn't* eat mouse pie. And I shall have to eat it, because it is a party. And *my* pie was going to be veal and ham. A pink and white pie-dish! and so is mine; just like Ribby's dishes; they were both bought at Tabitha Twitchit's."

Duchess went into her larder and took the pie off a shelf and looked at it.

"It is all ready to put into the oven. Such lovely pie-crust; and I put in a little tin patty-pan to hold up the crust; and I made a hole in the middle with a fork to let out the steam — Oh I do wish I could eat my own pie, instead of a pie made of mouse!"

Duchess considered and considered
and read Ribby's letter again —

"A pink and white pie-dish — and *you*
shall eat it *all*. 'You' means me — then
Ribby is not going to even taste the
pie herself? A pink and white pie-
dish! Ribby is sure to go out to buy
the muffins...Oh what a good idea!

Why shouldn't I rush along and put my pie into Ribby's oven when Ribby isn't there?"

Duchess was quite delighted with her own cleverness!

Ribby in the meantime had received Duchess's answer, and as soon as she was sure that the little dog could come — she popped *her* pie into the oven. There were two ovens, one above the other; some other knobs and handles were only ornamental and not intended to open. Ribby put the pie into the lower oven; the door was very stiff.

"The top oven bakes too quickly," said Ribby to herself. "It is a pie of the most delicate and tender mouse minced up with bacon. And I have taken out all the bones; because Duchess did nearly choke herself with a fish-bone last time I gave a party. She eats a little fast — rather big mouthfuls. But a most genteel and elegant little dog; infinitely superior company to Cousin Tabitha Twitchit."

THE PIE MADE OF MOUSE

Ribby put on some coal and swept
up the hearth. Then she went out with
a can to the well, for water to fill up
the kettle.

Then she began to set the room in
order, for it was the sitting-room as
well as the kitchen. She shook the
mats out at the front door and put
them straight; the hearth-rug was a
rabbit-skin. She dusted the clock and
the ornaments on the mantelpiece, and
she polished and rubbed the tables
and chairs.

Then she spread a very clean white
tablecloth, and set out her best china
tea-set, which she took out of a wall-
cupboard near the fire-place. The tea-
cups were white with a pattern of pink
roses; and the dinner-plates were white
and blue.

When Ribby had laid the table she took a jug and a blue and white dish, and went out down the field to the farm, to fetch milk and butter.

When she came back, she peeped into the bottom oven; the pie looked very comfortable.

Ribby put on her shawl and bonnet and went out again with a basket, to the village shop to buy a packet of tea, a pound of lump sugar, and a pot of marmalade.

And just at the same time, Duchess came out of *her* house, at the other end of the village.

Ribby met Duchess half-way down the street, also carrying a basket, covered with a cloth. They only bowed to one another; they did not speak, because they were going to have a party.

THE VEAL AND HAM PIE

As soon as Duchess had got round the corner out of sight — she simply ran! Straight away to Ribby's house!

Ribby went into the shop and bought what she required, and came out, after a pleasant gossip with Cousin Tabitha Twitchit.

Cousin Tabitha was disdainful afterwards in conversation —

"A little *dog* indeed! Just as if there were no CATS in Sawrey! And a *pie* for afternoon tea! The very idea!" said Cousin Tabitha Twitchit.

Ribby went on to Timothy Baker's and bought the muffins. Then she went home.

There seemed to be a sort of scuffling noise in the back passage, as she was coming in at the front door.

"I trust that is not that Pie; the spoons are locked up, however," said Ribby.

WHERE IS THE PIE MADE OF MOUSE?

But there was nobody there. Ribby opened the bottom oven door with some difficulty, and turned the pie. There began to be a pleasing smell of baked mouse!

Duchess in the meantime, had slipped out at the back door.

"It is a very odd thing that Ribby's pie was *not* in the oven when I put mine in! And I can't find it anywhere; I have looked all over the house. I put *my* pie into a nice hot oven at the top. I could not turn any of the other handles; I think that they are all shams," said Duchess, "but I wish I could have removed the pie made of mouse! I cannot think what she has done with it? I heard Ribby coming and I had to run out by the back door!"

Duchess went home and brushed her beautiful black coat; and then she picked a bunch of flowers in her garden as a present for Ribby; and passed the time until the clock struck four.

Ribby — having assured herself by careful search that there was really no one hiding in the cupboard or in the larder — went upstairs to change her dress.

She put on a lilac silk gown, for the party, and an embroidered muslin apron and tippet.

"It is very strange," said Ribby, "I did not *think* I left that drawer pulled out; has somebody been trying on my mittens?"

She came downstairs again, and
made the tea, and put the teapot on
the hob. She peeped again into the
bottom oven; the pie had become a
lovely brown, and it was steaming hot.

READY FOR THE PARTY

She sat down before the fire to wait for the little dog. "I am glad I used the *bottom* oven," said Ribby, "the top one would certainly have been very much too hot. I wonder why that cupboard door was open? Can there really have been someone in the house?"

Very punctually at four o'clock, Duchess started to go to the party. She ran so fast through the village that she was too early, and she had to wait a little while in the lane that leads down to Ribby's house.

"I wonder if Ribby has taken *my* pie out of the oven yet?" said Duchess, "and whatever can have become of the other pie made of mouse?"

At a quarter past four to the minute, there came a most genteel little tap-tappity. "Is Mrs. Ribston at home?" inquired Duchess in the porch.

DUCHESS IN THE PORCH

"Come in! and how do you do? my dear Duchess," cried Ribby. "I hope I see you well?"

"Quite well, I thank you, and how do *you* do, my dear Ribby?" said Duchess. "I've brought you some flowers; what a delicious smell of pie!"

"Oh, what lovely flowers! Yes, it is mouse and bacon!"

"Do not talk about food, my dear Ribby," said Duchess; "what a lovely white tea-cloth! . . . Is it done to a turn? Is it still in the oven?"

"I think it wants another five minutes," said Ribby. "Just a shade longer; I will pour out the tea, while we wait.

Do you take sugar, my dear Duchess?"

"Oh yes, please! my dear Ribby; and may I have a lump upon my nose?"

"With pleasure, my dear Duchess; how beautifully you beg! Oh, how sweetly pretty!"

Duchess sat up with the sugar on her nose and sniffed —

"How good that pie smells! I do love veal and ham — I mean to say mouse and bacon —"

She dropped the sugar in confusion, and had to go hunting under the tea-table, so she did not see which oven Ribby opened in order to get out the pie.

Ribby set the pie upon the table; there was a very savoury smell.

Duchess came out from under the tablecloth munching sugar, and sat up on a chair.

"I will first cut the pie for you; I am going to have muffin and marmalade," said Ribby.

"Do you really prefer muffin? Mind the patty-pan!"

"I beg your pardon?" said Ribby.

"May I pass you the marmalade?" said Duchess hurriedly.

The pie proved extremely toothsome, and the muffins light and hot. They disappeared rapidly, especially the pie!

"I think" — (thought the Duchess to herself) — "I *think* it would be wiser if I helped myself to pie; though Ribby did not seem to notice anything when she was cutting it. What very small fine pieces it has cooked into! I did not remember that I had minced it up so fine; I suppose this is a quicker oven than my own."

"How fast Duchess is eating!" thought Ribby to herself, as she buttered her fifth muffin.

The pie-dish was emptying rapidly! Duchess had had four helps already, and was fumbling with the spoon.

"A little more bacon, my dear Duchess?" said Ribby.

"Thank you, my dear Ribby; I was only feeling for the patty-pan."

"The patty-pan? my dear Duchess?"

WHERE IS THE PATTY-PAN?

"The patty-pan that held up the pie-crust," said Duchess, blushing under her black coat.

"Oh, I didn't put one in, my dear

Duchess," said Ribby; "I don't think
that it is necessary in pies made of
mouse."

Duchess fumbled with the spoon — "I
can't find it!" she said anxiously.

"There isn't a patty-pan," said Ribby,
looking perplexed.

"Yes, indeed, my dear Ribby; where
can it have gone to?" said Duchess.

"There most certainly is not one, my
dear Duchess. I disapprove of tin
articles in puddings and pies. It is
most undesirable — (especially when
people swallow in lumps!)" she added in
a lower voice.

Duchess looked very much alarmed,
and continued to scoop the inside of
the pie-dish.

"My Great-aunt Squintina (grand-mother of Cousin Tabitha Twitchit) — died of a thimble in a Christmas plum-pudding. *I* never put any article of metal in *my* puddings or pies."

Duchess looked aghast, and tilted up the pie-dish.

"I have only four patty-pans, and they are all in the cupboard."

Duchess set up a howl.

"I shall die! I shall die! I have swallowed a patty-pan! Oh, my dear Ribby, I do feel so ill!"

"It is impossible, my dear Duchess; there was not a patty-pan."

Duchess moaned and whined and rocked herself about.

"Oh I feel so dreadful, I have swallowed a patty-pan!"

"There was *nothing* in the pie," said Ribby severely.

"Yes there *was*, my dear Ribby, I am sure I have swallowed it!"

"Let me prop you up with a pillow, my dear Duchess; where do you think you feel it?"

"Oh I do feel so ill *all over* me, my dear Ribby; I have swallowed a large tin patty-pan with a sharp scalloped edge!"

"Shall I run for the doctor? I will just lock up the spoons!"

"Oh yes, yes! fetch Dr. Maggotty, my dear Ribby; he is a Pie himself, he will certainly understand."

Ribby settled Duchess in an armchair before the fire, and went out and hurried to the village to look for the doctor.

She found him at the smithy.

He was occupied in putting rusty nails into a bottle of ink, which he had obtained at the post office.

DR. MAGGOTTY'S MIXTURE

"Gammon? ha! Ha!" said he, with his head on one side.

Ribby explained that her guest had swallowed a patty-pan.

"Spinach? ha! HA!" said he, and accompanied her with alacrity.

He hopped so fast that Ribby had to run. It was most conspicuous. All the village could see that Ribby was fetching the doctor.

"I *knew* they would over-eat themselves!" said Cousin Tabitha Twitchit.

But while Ribby had been hunting for the doctor — a curious thing had happened to Duchess, who had been left by herself, sitting before the fire, sighing and groaning and feeling very unhappy.

"How *could* I have swallowed it! such a large thing as a patty-pan!"

She got up and went to the table, and felt inside the pie-dish again with a spoon.

"No; there is no patty-pan, and I put one in; and nobody has eaten pie except me, so I must have swallowed it!"

She sat down again, and stared mournfully at the grate. The fire crackled and danced, and something sizz-z-zled!

Duchess started! She opened the door of the *top* oven; out came a rich steamy flavour of veal and ham, and there stood a fine brown pie — and through a hole in the top of the pie-crust there was a glimpse of a little tin patty-pan!

Duchess drew a long breath —

"Then I must have been eating Mouse! . . . No wonder I feel ill . . . But perhaps I should feel worse if I had really swallowed a patty-pan!" Duchess reflected — "What a very awkward thing to have to explain to Ribby! I think I will put *my* pie in the back-yard and say nothing about it. When I go home, I will run round

and take it away." She put it outside the back door, and sat down again by the fire, and shut her eyes; when Ribby arrived with the doctor, she seemed fast asleep.

"Gammon, ha, HA?" said the doctor.

"I am feeling very much better," said Duchess, waking up with a jump.

"I am truly glad to hear it! He has brought you a pill, my dear Duchess!"

"I think I should feel *quite* well if he only felt my pulse," said Duchess, backing away from the magpie, who sidled up with something in his beak.

"It is only a bread-pill, you had much better take it; drink a little milk, my dear Duchess!"

"Gammon? Gammon?" said the doctor, while Duchess coughed and choked.

"Don't say that again!" said Ribby, losing her temper—"Here, take this bread and jam, and get out into the yard!"

"Gammon and Spinach! ha ha HA!" shouted Dr. Maggotty triumphantly outside the back door...

"I am feeling very much better, my dear Ribby," said Duchess. "Do you not think that I had better go home before it gets dark?"

"Perhaps it might be wise, my dear Duchess. I will lend you a nice warm shawl, and you shall take my arm."

"I would not trouble you for worlds; I feel wonderfully better. One pill of Dr. Maggotty —"

"Indeed it is most admirable, if it has cured you of a patty-pan! I will call directly after breakfast to ask how you have slept."

Ribby and Duchess said goodbye affectionately, and Duchess started home. Half-way up the lane she stopped and looked back; Ribby had gone in and shut her door. Duchess slipped through the fence, and ran round to the back of Ribby's house and peeped into the yard.

Upon the roof of the pig-stye sat Dr. Maggotty and three jackdaws. The jackdaws were eating pie-crust, and the magpie was drinking gravy out of a patty-pan.

SO THERE REALLY *WAS* A PATTY-PAN

"Gammon, ha, Ha!" he shouted when he saw Duchess's little black nose peeping round the corner.

Duchess ran home feeling uncommonly silly!

When Ribby came out for a pailful of water to wash up the tea-things, she found a pink and white pie-dish lying smashed in the middle of the yard. The patty-pan was under the pump, where Dr. Maggotty had considerately left it.

Ribby stared with amazement — "Did you ever see the like! so there really *was* a patty-pan? . . . But *my* patty-pans are all in the kitchen cupboard. Well I never did! . . . Next time I want to give a party — I will invite Cousin Tabitha Twitchit!"

THE TALE OF
JOHNNY TOWN-MOUSE

JOHNNY TOWN-MOUSE was born in a cupboard. Timmy Willie was born in a garden. Timmy Willie was a little country mouse who went to town by mistake in a hamper. The gardener sent vegetables to town once a week by carrier; he packed them in a big hamper.

THE gardener left the hamper by
the garden gate, so that the carrier
could pick it up when he passed.
Timmy Willie crept in through a hole
in the wickerwork, and after eating
some peas — Timmy Willie fell fast
asleep.

HE awoke in a fright, while the
hamper was being lifted into the
carrier's cart. Then there was a jolting,
and a clattering of horse's feet; other
packages were thrown in; for miles
and miles — jolt — jolt — jolt! and Timmy
Willie trembled amongst the jumbled
up vegetables.

AT last the cart stopped at a house,
where the hamper was taken out,
carried in, and set down. The cook
gave the carrier sixpence; the back
door banged, and the cart rumbled
away. But there was no quiet; there
seemed to be hundreds of carts passing.
Dogs barked; boys whistled in the
street; the cook laughed, the parlour
maid ran up and down-stairs; and a
canary sang like a steam engine.

TIMMY WILLIE, who had lived all his life in a garden, was almost frightened to death. Presently the cook opened the hamper and began to unpack the vegetables. Out sprang the terrified Timmy Willie.

UP jumped the cook on a chair, exclaiming "A mouse! a mouse! Call the cat! Fetch me the poker, Sarah!" Timmy Willie did not wait for Sarah with the poker; he rushed along the skirting-board till he came to a little hole, and in he popped.

HE dropped half a foot, and crashed into the middle of a mouse dinner party, breaking three glasses. —"Who in the world is this?" inquired Johnny Town-mouse. But after the first exclamation of surprise he instantly recovered his manners.

WITH the utmost politeness he
introduced Timmy Willie to nine
other mice, all with long tails and
white neckties. Timmy Willie's own
tail was insignificant. Johnny Town-
mouse and his friends noticed it; but
they were too well bred to make
personal remarks; only one of them
asked Timmy Willie if he had ever
been in a trap?

THE dinner was of eight courses; not much of anything, but truly elegant. All the dishes were unknown to Timmy Willie, who would have been a little afraid of tasting them; only he was very hungry, and very anxious to behave with company manners. The continual noise upstairs made him so nervous, that he dropped a plate. "Never mind, they don't belong to us," said Johnny.

"WHY don't those youngsters come back with the dessert?" It should be explained that two young mice, who were waiting on the others, went skirmishing upstairs to the kitchen between courses. Several times they had come tumbling in, squeaking and laughing; Timmy Willie learnt with horror that they were being chased by the cat. His appetite failed, he felt faint. "Try some jelly?" said Johnny Town-mouse.

"NO? Would you rather go to bed? I will show you a most comfortable sofa pillow."

The sofa pillow had a hole in it. Johnny Town-mouse quite honestly recommended it as the best bed, kept exclusively for visitors. But the sofa smelt of cat. Timmy Willie preferred to spend a miserable night under the fender.

IT was just the same next day. An
excellent breakfast was provided — for
mice accustomed to eat bacon; but
Timmy Willie had been reared on
roots and salad. Johnny Town-mouse
and his friends racketted about under
the floors, and came boldly out all
over the house in the evening. One
particularly loud crash had been caused
by Sarah tumbling downstairs with the
tea-tray; there were crumbs and sugar
and smears of jam to be collected, in
spite of the cat.

TIMMY WILLIE longed to be at
home in his peaceful nest in a
sunny bank. The food disagreed with
him; the noise prevented him from
sleeping. In a few days he grew so
thin that Johnny Town-mouse noticed
it, and questioned him. He listened to
Timmy Willie's story and inquired
about the garden. "It sounds rather
a dull place? What do you do when
it rains?"

"WHEN it rains, I sit in my little sandy burrow and shell corn and seeds from my Autumn store. I peep out at the throstles and blackbirds on the lawn, and my friend Cock Robin. And when the sun comes out again, you should see my garden and the flowers — roses and pinks and pansies — no noise except the birds and bees, and the lambs in the meadows."

"THERE goes that cat again!" exclaimed Johnny Town-mouse. When they had taken refuge in the coal-cellar he resumed the conversation; "I confess I am a little disappointed; we have endeavoured to entertain you, Timothy William."

"Oh yes, yes, you have been most kind; but I do feel so ill," said Timmy Willie.

"IT may be that your teeth and digestion are unaccustomed to our food; perhaps it might be wiser for you to return in the hamper."

"Oh? Oh!" cried Timmy Willie.

"Why of course for the matter of that we could have sent you back last week," said Johnny rather huffily — "did you not know that the hamper goes back empty on Saturdays?"

So Timmie Willie said goodbye to his new friends, and hid in the hamper with a crumb of cake and a withered cabbage leaf; and after much jolting, he was set down safely in his own garden.

SOMETIMES on Saturdays he went
to look at the hamper lying by the
gate, but he knew better than to get
in again. And nobody got out, though
Johnny Town-mouse had half promised
a visit.

THE winter passed; the sun came out again; Timmy Willie sat by his burrow warming his little fur coat, and sniffing the smell of violets and spring grass. He had nearly forgotten his visit to town. When up the sandy path all spick and span with a brown leather bag came Johnny Town-mouse!

TIMMY WILLIE received him with open arms. "You have come at the best of all the year, we will have herb pudding and sit in the sun."

"H'm'm! it is a little damp," said Johnny Town-mouse, who was carrying his tail under his arm, out of the mud.

WHAT is that fearful noise?" he started violently.

"That?" said Timmy Willie, "that is only a cow; I will beg a little milk, they are quite harmless, unless they happen to lie down upon you. How are all our friends?"

JOHNNY'S account was rather middling. He explained why he was paying his visit so early in the season; the family had gone to the sea-side for Easter; the cook was doing spring cleaning, on board wages, with particular instructions to clear out the mice. There were four kittens, and the cat had killed the canary.

"THEY say we did it; but I know better," said Johnny Town-mouse. "Whatever is that fearful racket?"

"That is only the lawnmower; I will fetch some of the grass clippings presently to make your bed. I am sure you had better settle in the country, Johnny."

"H'M'M — we shall see by Tuesday week; the hamper is stopped while they are at the sea-side."

"I am sure you will never want to live in town again," said Timmy Willie.

BUT he did. He went back in the very next hamper of vegetables; he said it was too quiet!!

ONE place suits one person, another place suits another person. For my part, I prefer to live in the country, like Timmy Willie.